Innocence

It was my 18th birthday living in a quiet rich community in Arlington, Texas with my adoptive parents Kaitlin and Kyle. They are amazing adoptive parents and very proud of me in my final year of high school.

Kaitlin and Kyle took me to an exclusive restaurant with a private room for dinner. Kaitlin and Kyle are a very wealthy couple. Kyle is a software engineer and Kaitlin is a stay at home wife.

We were talking like normal when Kaitlin got up wished me a happy birthday then gave me a gift from under the table. Kaitlin said you have grown into a fine young man since we adopted you. She hugged me, which surprised me since she has never hugged me before since I was adopted.

I never really thought about it since it never happened before I said thanks for the gift Kaitlin and I opened it. It was a brand-new gold Rolex, I said oh wow thank you again. Kaitlin said try it on see if it fits. I put it on and it fit. I was surprised and happy. I hate watches moving around on my wrist.

It was Kyle's turn, he said I know you have your driver's license but no car so here you go. He gave me a key for an Audi and said it's a brand-new Audi A4. I said oh my god thank you so much. I really appreciate this and hugged him.

Kyle said I had it delivered while we are here at your birthday dinner. We finally ordered and the meal came 10 minutes later. We ate very well this birthday night of mine. I was all smiles and so was Kyle and Kaitlin.

After dinner we went home and in the driveway was a brand-new Audi A4 with a red bow, black in color. I said thank you guys again this is the best birthday ever. We took the bow off and I hopped in the driver's seat.

Kaitlin climbed in the passenger seat and Kyle got in the back. They both said let's take your new car for a spin around the neighborhood. I slowly backed out using the camera. I drove us around the neighborhood that I know pretty well after years of living here.

I went at the posted speed limit of 25 mph for a few miles then took us back home. I said I guess Kaitlin won't be taking me to school anymore. Kaitlin said you have a car now and I smiled saying yes, I do.

I was thinking my friends are going to die when they see me pull up in my new car. They all have cars except for me. I could not wait for Monday. It came up before I noticed. I couldn't sleep that night.

I was ready to drive after I sat and had breakfast with Kyle and Kaitlin. They both said drive carefully no speeding. I told them that I would follow all posted speed limits. I did follow it on the way to school.

When I arrived at school, there was a lot of my friends outside. I parked and got out of the car. I heard screaming and people saying oh my god you finally got a car. I said yep it's about damn time. I got some hi fives and hugs. We went to class and I was smiling the whole day. I drove back home in one piece parked and got out of the car.

I told Kaitlin that I was home and she made my usual snack after school. Kaitlin said how was school and I told her. She said how was driving to school, I said great no problems. I drove the speed limit and she was very happy to hear that, then she hugged me again.

Kaitlin said Kyle had to go on travel for work. I said it's just you and me. I went to my room and did my homework. When I was finished, I came down and hung out with Kaitlin until it was bedtime.

I took a shower, brushed my teeth and flossed with my Waterpik. I climbed into bed and was about to fall asleep when I heard a knock on the door. I said come in Kaitlin. She opened the door and came into my room. I saw her in a sexy nightgown. I was thinking oh wow, she is a beautiful woman.

I hope I marry a goddess like her one day. Kaitlin said do you mind if I sleep here tonight. I said no, I don't mind hop in, there is plenty of room in this king size bed.

Kaitlin climbed in and we both closed our eyes and went to sleep. During the night, I felt Kaitlin glued to me. I could feel her big melons on my back and her warm pussy on my ass. I enjoyed it and went back to sleep.

I woke up and she was still glued to me. Kaitlin said you don't mind do you baby. I said no problem it feels good. Kaitlin said cool do you mind if I sleep here until Kyle gets back. I said no problem happy to cuddle with you.

Kaitlin giggled and said you're the best. I said I need to get ready for school. She said right and I'll go make us breakfast. I said thanks and 20 minutes later I went down to eat breakfast with the lovely Kaitlin.

I said I'm leaving for school and she hugged me with her awesome body. I went to school thinking what is Kaitlin up to with all of these hugs and sleeping in my bed. I couldn't wait until bedtime arrived. I got ready for bed and came out of the bathroom. Kaitlin was already in my bed with a smile on her face.

I climbed in and Kaitlin hugged me from behind and we went to sleep. I slept well; I woke because Kaitlin was stroking my hard cock. I moaned and said that feels so good don't stop. Kaitlin said do you like my hand job.

I said so that is what it called. Kaitlin said so have you had a girl give you a hand job before and I said no, I'm a virgin and I haven't been kissed either. Kaitlin said really so you have not had sex yet. I said no. Kaitlin said oh wow didn't see that coming. I said will you teach me how to kiss.

Kaitlin said I like your big black cock. I said thanks have you held a big black cock before and Kaitlin said no this was the first time I've seen or held a big black cock. Kaitlin said since its early let's practice kissing.

Kaitlin gave me a peck on the lips. She said now you try and I gave her a peck on the lips. Kaitlin said this is a French kiss, then she kissed me and pushed her tongue in my mouth. I rubbed my tongue on her tongue as we held the kiss.

hair. She sucked me for a while until I felt something I never felt before and I let myself go. Kaitlin swallowed it all and I said wow did you swallow all of my sperm.

Kaitlin said yeah, sometimes a naughty woman like me will swallow a man's sperm to turn him on. Kaitlin said did you like your first blow job. I said hell yeah, it was great, you can do that anytime. Kaitlin said cool, I love to suck cock.

I said will you show me how to eat pussy. Kaitlin said of course, come with me lets go to your bedroom. Kaitlin took off all her clothes and laid down with her legs open. A naked Kaitlin is a stunning visual beauty which overwhelmed me with lust for her completely.

I crawled between her legs; I ran my hands gently over her sweet white thighs. I said your thighs are beautiful and she said thanks sweetie. Kaitlin said some girls like their pussy eating and some girls like to be fingered. I personally like my pussy fingered but I'll show you how to eat my pussy too.

I laid down right at the entrance to her beautiful white pussy. She instructed me to lick up and down her pink slit which I did. The smell of her pussy was intoxicating. Kaitlin said this is my clit, lick it gently with your tongue, then squeeze it with your lips. I did it until I got the hang of it then she said harder. I did it harder for a while and Kaitlin scream oh fuck you're really good at that, she held my head and her whole body vibrated.

I said did you have an orgasm. Kaitlin said oh yeah, you are so good to your white mommy. I said can I finger you too. Kaitlin said give me a minute. I need to come down from my orgasm high. A few minutes later, she took my hand and sucked my middle finger like she sucked my dick.

After a little bit she said stick it in my pussy, baby. I pushed my black finger in Kaitlin's white pussy. Kaitlin started moaning immediately, she said I love this anytime you want to finger me go for it baby. I said I will do that for you anytime I want.

Kaitlin said cool, it always gets me hot, sucking a dick also gets me hot too. I started fingering her pussy slowly at first. Kaitlin moaned louder then said faster. I sped up my fingering of her pussy at warp speed.

Kaitlin said oh god I'm coming again. I smiled because I brought her to full pleasure again. Kaitlin pulled me to her face and kissed me passionately. She said this stays between us no one can know our interracial passion for each other not even Kyle. I said it will be our private secret forever.

Kaitlin said that's my baby. I massaged her big titties. She said you like my big titties. I said oh yeah, they are beautiful. She said do you want to suck them for me. I said hell yeah. She said go for it baby. I grabbed her big tits and started sucking like a hungry animal. Kaitlin loved it then she told me to bite her nipples. I bit her nipples and she said harder. I bit her harder and she moaned oh yeah.

Kaitlin said there is one more thing I want to show you. She said put your cock between my tits, I said what is this called. She said this how you tit fuck a girl with big titties like me. I put my dick between her tits and she squeezed my dick with her big titties. Kaitlin said slide it back and forth. I started sliding my hard-black cock between her big white titties and man that felt really good.

I fucked her big titties for a long time then I felt an orgasm. I held my cock and sprayed her tits with my orgasm milk. I accidentally hit Kaitlin in the face with some of my sperm. She wiped it off and ate it. Kaitlin ate my cum off her tits too, it was highly erotic to watch her do it.

I said you are the best; do you want to go to prom with me since I don't have a date. Kaitlin said sure I'd love to go to prom with you. I said thank you so much. I hugged and kissed her. Kaitlin said we will have to behave in public no kissing. I said I totally understand. I said I will be at the prom with the most beautiful woman in the world.

Kaitlin said you are so sweet to say that about me baby. I love you and I said I love you too Kaitlin. Kaitlin said do you want to watch me take a shower. I said that would be awesome. We went to my bathroom. I stood and watched as Kaitlin took a sexy shower soaping up her entire delicious body for my viewing pleasure. I loved every second of it when she asked me to soap up her back. I was very happy to soap up her back and I soaped up her juicy ass too.

She said thanks baby and rinsed off. I wrapped a towel around her when she got out of the shower. That weekend we went to find Kaitlin a prom dress and I had to buy a tuxedo. The prom was a week away and Kyle was still on travel. Kaitlin told him that I was taking her to the prom and he taught it was a sweet gesture.

The night of the prom we set up the camera and took a ton of beautiful pictures of us. We heard the limousine horn beep. We stopped and walked to the car holding hands. When we arrived, we showed our invitations and went into the ballroom.

I introduced Kaitlin to my friends and teachers. I looked around but Kelli the girl that I have been in love with for 4 years of High School was nowhere to be seen.

So, Kaitlin and I danced smiling at each other the whole night long. I became hard as we danced.

Kaitlin said lots of high schoolers lose their virginity on prom night, do you want to make love to me tonight so I can make you a man.

I said that would be great to lose my virginity to a goddess. Kaitlin giggled and said you say the sweetest things to me. I said I love you sexy Kaitlin. She said I love you too baby. After prom, I said goodbye to my friends and teachers. Kaitlin and I rolled out of there in our limousine.

When we got home, Kaitlin said wait here. I need to get ready for your big night. Fifteen minutes later, Kaitlin said come to the guest bedroom one. I went up and opened the door. There was candles everywhere. Kaitlin was in the middle of the bed in the sexiest lingerie that I've ever seen from Victoria secret.

I said wow Kaitlin, you look amazing. She said why thank you kind sir please remove your tuxedo. I dropped that tuxedo like a bad habit. I climbed onto Kaitlin and kissed her passionately. We held each other and kissed for a long time.

Kaitlin said take my panties off. I gently removed her panties savoring the moment. I kissed her sweet white thighs then moved to her clit. I sucked and squeezed it with my lips to give Kaitlin immense pleasure.

After she came, Kaitlin said give me your cock. I pushed it in her pretty mouth and she sucked it really good for me. She stopped and said time to lose your virginity to your white mommy. I gathered myself between her sweet white thighs. I put my black cock at the entrance to her white pussy.

I pushed my black cock in her white pussy forcefully. It went in with much effort. Kaitlin moaned oh my god you have a big cock. I kissed her and she wrapped her legs around me as I massaged her tight white pussy with my black cock.

To me it was the best feeling that I've ever had in my life. I never knew losing my virginity would feel this good. Kaitlin kissed my neck as I gave it to her harder and harder. It just felt better and better as I fucked Kaitlin. I felt her pussy vibrate on my cock as she screamed out loud with pleasure. I knew she came on my cock.

Kaitlin said let's try another position. I pulled out of Kaitlin pleasure heaven and she bent over and said this is doggie my favorite position. I strongly pushed my cock back in her pleasure center. I held her sexy wide hips. I slowly fucked her for a while then she said you can fuck me harder. So, I started pounding the shit out of her.

Oh, what a glorious feeling to take her sexy wide hips to pound her hard. I gave it to her mercilessly until I couldn't hold back my pleasure anymore. I let my sperm flow rapidly into Kaitlin's white vagina as my eyes rolled back in my head.

Kaitlin turned around and kissed me passionately. She said now you're a man as we lay beside each other holding hands. I said that was the best thing ever. Kaitlin said I'm glad your first time is with me. I said I am glad it's with you too. I said thanks for making my first-time special Kaitlin. She said it was my pleasure besides your big cock gave me a lot of pleasure too.

Kaitlin and I slept naked together in the guest room. I woke up first and watched her pretty face as she slept. When she woke up, I said good morning beautiful lover of mine. Kaitlin smiled and said good morning my handsome stud.

Kyle came back from his long business trip just in time for graduation. Kaitlin and Kyle were going to be at my graduation from high school. I was very happy about it. Graduation day came and I was nervous. I walked across the aisle to cheers and music. After graduation, I was in the parking lot congratulating my friends.

I got a tap on the shoulder and it was Kelli. The sexiest vanilla goddess that I have been in love with for four years and never got up the courage to ask her out. She lives like two blocks from my house. I walked by her house many times hoping to see her but I never did.

I said hi Kelli, she said hi and congratulations. She hugged me tight to my surprise and pleasure. Kelli gave me a peck on the lips which made my day. She said see you around and turned to leave.

I said wait a second. I held her pretty face gently and kissed her passionately in front of everyone.

It lasted for quite a while, it felt like I was floating and in heaven at the same time. When we came up for air. We looked at each other smiling and very happy. I said can I text you sometime. Kelli said sure and we exchanged numbers.

We both heard someone say that was some kiss. We both spun around, it was Kaitlin and Kyle. Both were smiling looking at me very proud. I said this is Kelli, I've only been in love with her for 4 years but we never spoke until today. Kelli said the feeling is mutual.

Kelli and I hugged again, she gave me a peck on the lips and said text me. She left to go back to her family. Kyle and Kaitlin took pictures of me in my cap and gown. Kaitlin said I took pictures of you two lovebirds. I smiled at her and she said let's go to dinner.

All three of us went to my graduation dinner. It was surreal, I can't believe that I graduated and will be going to the University of Texas. Kaitlin asked if I got Kelli's number. I said yeah, I'll text her later. We ate and talked about my future. I hoped it involved Kelli.

A few days later, I text Kelli and she replied. I was happy. We started texting back and forth. I found out that she was going to University of Texas too. I said that is great, I'm going there too. I asked her if she wanted to come over. Kelli said sure.

When she came over, I was nervous. It was just Kaitlin and me. Kyle was back on the road again. I met her at the door and she looked nervous too. I hugged and kissed her on the lips. I introduced her officially to Kaitlin. Kelli said you are very beautiful to my white mommy Kaitlin.

We sat and talked for a little bit with Kaitlin. Kelli's sweet white thighs were giving me the vapors. Kaitlin said you guys can go to his room you are both 18 years old. I said ok and took Kelli up to my room. She looked around then said nice room.

I said thank you Kelli. I can't believe that you are in my room and that I kissed you. Kelli said why is that so hard to believe. I said I dig you a lot. Kelli said I dig you too. I was hoping that you asked me to the prom. I said I looked for you at the prom but I didn't see you. Kelli said I didn't go because I didn't have a date and I didn't want to go alone.

Kelli said who did you go with, I said I went with Kaitlin. Kelli said ok, you had me worried for a second that you went with someone from our school. I said the only girl that I liked at that high school is hot Kelli. She laughed out loud when I said it. I smiled at her.

Kelli said since we are alone do you want to make out. I said sure I like kissing you. We sat on the bed and hugged each other. We started making out and it was steamy. We kissed for a long time then we laid on my bed holding hands.

Kelli said I want to be your full-time girlfriend. I said I want to be your full-time boyfriend. Its settle then we are two peas in a pod. Kelli laughed then kissed me. She said you can come over to my house too. I said ok tomorrow.

The next day I went over to her house. I met her mom Krystal. She gave me a warm welcome with a hug. We sat and talked for a little bit then Kelli said we will be in my bedroom. She took me by the hand to her room.

It was a beautiful room; she had a picture of us at graduation kissing each other. Kelli said my mom took a picture of us. I said cool I felt like I was floating when we kissed. Kelli giggled and said me too, I've wanted to kiss you for a long time.

I said tell me about it. I was looking at Kelli's big titties when she said do you want to see my big tits. I said oh yeah. She giggled and opened her shirt. Kelli took her bra off and I said damn, those are beautiful. Kelli giggled and I said can I touch them. She said sure, I gently massaged her big titties.

I leaned in and sucked on her nipples gently. Kelli moaned as I sucked on both of her big titties. She said can I see your dick. I said sure and took my pants off then my boxers. Kelli said oh wow that's a big cock, good thing those bitches at our high school didn't know about your big cock.

I said why, Kelli said they would have wanted to fuck you. Kelli grabbed my cock and started stroking my cock. It felt absolutely wonderful then she said do you want a blow job. I said sure baby, Kelli leaned down and started sucking my black cock. I couldn't believe what was happening.

Kelli was really good at sucking my cock. I said can I eat your pussy. Kelli said sure although I've had sex before no guy has eating my pussy before. I said I'm happy to be the first. Kelli giggled and laid back. I started by kissing her sweet white thighs. I licked up and down her shaved pink pussy. I fingered her pussy and sucked on her clit.

Kelli said oh wow that feels really good don't stop. I kept at it until Kelli said oh god I'm coming. I stopped and she said wow that was a great experience that you may repeat. Kelli said do you want to have sex since we did everything else.

I said sure. She said don't worry I'm on birth control. I don't want kids until I'm married. I said cool safer sex. Kelli giggled as I stroked my hard cock rubbing it on her pussy. She said be gentle you have a really big cock. I said I will be gentle. I slowly pushed and pushed my cock into wet Kelli.

I finally got all the way in balls deep. She said oh wow I feel totally full. I started pumping slowly massaging her vagina with my hard penis. I squeezed her big titties as I fucked Kelli for the first time.

I saw Kelli's eyes roll back in her head and I knew what to expect. I saw her lubricate my cock with her pleasure milk. I said do you want to try doggie. Kelli said sure I know you just want to play with my big ass. I said I love your big ass.

Kelli bent over and jiggled it for me. I playfully smacked her sexy ass and massaged it. I penetrated her pussy again. I held her hips and gave it to her. She moaned oh god I love your big cock so good to my pussy. I loved watching her big booty jiggle on my cock. I smacked it and she creamed my cock again.

I gave it to her faster and I couldn't hold it any longer, I spilled my seed in my hot new girlfriend

Kelli for the first time. Damn it felt good to release in her as I massaged her juicy ass.

We laid beside each other smiling, I said that was fun. Kelli said that was hot and very pleasurable thanks for making me cum twice. I said my pleasure pretty Kelli. She smiled and said thank you my handsome stud.

I said we should take a nap together let's set an alarm on our phones for 30 minutes. We cuddled up naked smiling at each other and went to sleep. We woke up thirty minutes later totally refreshed.

Kelli put on a sexy little silk robe. She said I'll walk you out. I put back on my clothes and got ready to go back home. We went downstairs, Krystal was being nosy asking what were you two doing up there.

Kelli said I had great interracial sex with my black boyfriend, he fucked my brains out, ejaculating his sperm in my white vagina. I said your hot daughter has a wonderful vagina and great mouth for sucking black cock.

Krystal said oh my I'm very excited that my daughter got some black cock in her. She hugged me tight and said welcome to the family. I said I look forward too many years with your daughter.

Kelli said I look forward to giving it up to my black stud for many years. I laughed out loud and so did her mom. Kelli walked me to the door, we kissed and I walked home in shock from that conversation.

When I arrived home, Kaitlin was waiting for me. She said did you fuck Kelli. I said yes, I fucked Kelli. Kaitlin said now you have two notches in your belt, me and Kelli. I said your funny. Kaitlin giggled and I said you don't mind me having a girlfriend do you.

Kaitlin said we are still going to fuck aren't we. I said hell yeah, I'm never giving up your sweet white pussy. Kaitlin said that's my baby. We sat on the couch. Kaitlin kissed me then pulled me on top of her. She said fuck me with your dirty cock from your girlfriend Kelli.

Oh my god, I couldn't believe she said that but it really turned me on a lot. I pulled her robe open and she was totally naked I slammed my cock deep in her cunt. I started pounding away at her pussy.

We both started moaning like crazy as we intensely fucked like savages. We kissed passionately and held each other tight, I gave Kaitlin the business, I pounded her sexy ass into the fucking couch.

Kaitlin said oh yeah, I missed your big cock as I felt her horny pussy lubricated my cock and 5 minutes later. I spilled my seed in her horny ass pussy. We kissed and held each other in love on the couch.

Kaitlin said your white mommy will always love you even if you have a girlfriend. I said I know that I'll always love and want you too.

Kelli and I attended Texas University for four years then we both graduated with a degree in accounting. We started our careers at the same accounting firm.

A few years into our professional lives, Kelli said I want to have your baby and get married. I said hot Kelli will you do me the honor of marrying me.

I retrieved a ring from under the mattress. Kelli said oh my god, you have a ring. I said I've had one since we started our professional careers. I said don't be mad, I had help from Kaitlin. Kelli said I don't mind my mother in law has great taste when she saw the ring.

Kelli put the ring on and it fit. We called Kelli's parents and told them the wonderful news. We called Kyle and Kaitlin to give them the great news. Both of our families were happy.

We had a little ceremony at the courthouse with Kelli's parents along with Kyle and Kaitlin. We honeymooned at a wonderful resort in Arizona. Kelli said I'm not on birth control anymore time for you to impregnate your horny wifey.

I said I love you and I can't wait to be your baby daddy. Kelli took all of her clothes off and I took my clothes off too. We jumped into the bed and had an intense make out session. I kissed my way down to her big tits, I sucked them good then tasted her sweet white pussy. Kelli said my turn and sucked the hell out of my cock.

She held my black cock and slid down my black pole. I squeezed her big tits as Kelli fucked my black cock with her white pussy. Kelli moaned and said my first orgasm on my husband's big black cock. A second later I felt the lubrication of her pleasure milk.

Kelli bent over and said impregnate your wifey. I said with pleasure slamming my cock up her horny cunt. I held her hips and showed her no mercy on her sweet white pussy. After a good amount of pounding, I moaned and said here comes my baby making seed.

I emptied my balls into my hot wife Kelli. She put a pillow under her back to keep my sperm in her vagina. I smiled and said I hope you get pregnant. I can't wait to fuck you silly when your pregnant.

Kelli said I can't wait for you to rub my big belly and fuck me with your big black cock.

Kelli and I fucked like bunnies the whole week of our honeymoon. We were both sore as shit when we went back home.

A couple of months later, Kelli started gaining weight so we suspected that she was pregnant. We both went to her doctor and they did the test. She was pregnant and they confirmed it with a blood test.

3 month later Kelli told her parents. I called and told Kaitlin and Kyle. They were very happy especially Kaitlin. She started bringing over baby stuff all the time. We didn't have to buy any baby stuff.

4 months later when baby Caroline was born to me and Kelly after 4 hours of labor. She came out screaming like crazy. We left the hospital after a few days; both sets of parents were waiting for us as we arrived home.

They were very excited to see baby Caroline. I was happy to see them too. During their stay Kaitlin volunteer to stay with us and to help take care of the baby when we go back to work.

I said are you sure Kaitlin. She said I'm sure I don't want some stranger taking care of my granddaughter. We said ok and thank you so much. I was happy someone I knew will be taking care of my daughter.

The first day we left baby Caroline with Kaitlin after being off for a month of leave. I came home alone. Kelli had to work late. Kaitlin greeted me at the door.

She said where is Kelli. I said she is working late today; she will be home in a couple of hours. I said where is baby Caroline. Kaitlin said I just put her down for a nap.

Kaitlin kissed me passionately up against the door. I grabbed her fat ass squeezing it tight. She jumped on my hips. I dropped my pants and took my hard cock out. Kaitlin slid down my black pole.

Kaitlin moaned oh how I've missed your big black cock in my white pussy. I said I miss your horny cunt too. I kissed her neck as I jack hammered her pussy. I put her against the door and fucked her harder.

Kaitlin moaned yes, fuck me harder. I fucked her harder. Kaitlin released her cream on my cock. I felt the lubrication and it spurred me on greatly. I gave it to her hard and balls deep. I felt maximum pressure and I release my seed into Kaitlin.

We held each other and kissed passionately. I said that was great Kaitlin, I love you and missed you. Kaitlin said I love you and missed you too baby.

We heard the baby crying; we fixed our clothes and both of us went up to get baby Caroline. Kaitlin picked her up and held her until she stopped crying. I said I've fantasized about knocking you up Kaitlin.

Kaitlin said that would be hot but Kyle would kill us both when he sees the headline rich white woman knocked up by her handsome black adopted son.

The end

www.ingramcontent.com/pod-product-compliance
Lightning Source LLC
LaVergne TN
LVHW052113160826
845678LV00015B/3527
9798756719383